10/13

*squeak
squeak*

WHAT FLOATS IN A MOAT?

For John
—L. B.

For Julie and Romy
—M. C.

WHAT FLOATS IN A MOAT?

- by - LYNNE BERRY ✦ ✦ ✦ ✦ - illustrated by - MATTHEW CORDELL

Simon & Schuster Books for Young Readers
NEW YORK   LONDON   TORONTO   SYDNEY   NEW DELHI

Archie the Goat
stopped short at a moat.

He measured and mapped.

He doodled and drew.
He sketched and scribbled
and scrawled.

"*Aha!* To cross the moat,"
 pronounced the goat,
"we build a contraption to float!"

"Or," said Skinny the Hen, "we could just take
   the drawbridge."

"Bah," said Archie," drawbridge, straw-bridge."

"This is no time for a drawbridge. This is a time
   for science!"

"Right!" said the hen. "Science!"

The hen and the goat, alongside the moat, took stock of their cart of supplies.

"A barrel might float," mused the goat. "We begin with a barrel of buttermilk!"

The hen and the goat, alongside the moat,
hammered and nailed, clanged and banged.

They wired and tied, and built the SS *Buttermilk*.

Archie the Goat climbed aboard. "Ready for launch?" he called.

"Ready," said Skinny the Hen.

"Push!" said Archie the Goat.
"I *am* pushing," said Skinny.

"Shove!" said Archie the Goat.
"I *am* shoving," said Skinny.

"Heave!" said Archie the Goat.
"I *am* heaving," said Skinny.
"Heave-*UMPH!*"

The barrel and goat splashed into the moat—

GLUB GLUB

and sank.

Archie the Goat dripped out of the moat.

"Take note, take note," pronounced the goat, "a barrel might *not* float."

"Apparently not," said the hen. "Shall we take the drawbridge, then?"

"Bah," said Archie, "drawbridge, flaw-bridge." "This is no time for a drawbridge. This is a time for science!"

"Hmm," said the hen. "Science."

Archie the Goat gazed at the moat.

He puzzled and pondered.

He doodled and drew.

He sketched
and scribbled
and scrawled.

"Aha! To cross the moat," pronounced the goat,
"an *empty* barrel might float!"

"Empty?" said Skinny.

"Empty," said Archie. "Drink, Skinny, drink!"

"Drink *buttermilk*?" asked Skinny.

"Indeed," said Archie. "For science!"

"Ha!" said Skinny. "YOU are the scientist."

"Ah," said Archie, "but YOU are skinny."

Skinny held her nose, and started to slurp. *"Blech!"*

She guzzled. She gulped.

She sipped and slurped and guzzled . . .
and sipped and slurped and gulped . . .
and sipped and slurped and guzzled . . .
to the bottom of a barrel of buttermilk.

"Ugh."

"Bah," said Archie.

Then goat and hen hammered and nailed,

clanged and banged.

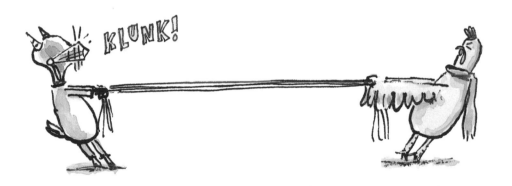

They wired and tied, and built the SS *Empty*.

Archie the Goat climbed aboard.
"Ready for launch?" he called.

"Ready," said Not-So-Skinny the Hen. "Heave-*HO*!"

The barrel, with goat, splashed into the moat—
and floated!

And tipped . . .

and rolled . . .

and tossed the goat
into the moat.

Archie the Goat dripped out of the moat.

"Take note, take note," pronounced the goat,
"indeed, a barrel does float!"

"And yet," said Skinny the Hen, "we remain
outside the moat."

"Bah," said Archie, "we try again, Skinny the Hen."

"Again?" groaned the hen.

"Indeed," said Archie, "the third and final barrel. Drink, Skinny, drink!"

The hen sighed. The hen sipped.
The hen sighed. The hen slurped.

She guzzled. She gulped. She stopped.
She could not drink another drop.

TAP!
TAP!

"Ah," said Archie, "just right!"

CLANG

BANG!

The hen and the goat, alongside the moat, hammered and nailed, clanged and banged.

They wired and tied, and built the SS *Ballast*.

Archie the Goat climbed aboard. "Ready for launch?" he called. "Ready," said Skinny the Hen.

BURP

S.S. BALLAST

"Heave, heave, heave-UMPH!"

The barrel, with goat, splashed into the moat —

and sank—

but floated.

SANK AND

FLOATED

"Eureka!" said Archie the Goat. And he paddled across the moat—just in time to meet the queen hurrying from the castle.

"Archimedes?" called the queen. "For Pete's sake, next time, *take the drawbridge*! And *where* is the rest of my buttermilk?"

"In the moat," pronounced the goat.

"And in the hen," moaned the hen.

"All," said Archie, "in the name of science."

"Science?" fussed the queen. "*Science?* What about my *buttermilk?*"

"Bah," said Archie, "buttermilk, gutter-milk."
"This is no time for deliveries. This is time for discoveries!"

"Indeed," said Skinny the Hen.

– AUTHOR'S NOTE –

What a relief that Archie's barrel finally floated! And thanks to Archimedes, a famous Greek scientist (and Archie's namesake!) we know why.

Archimedes found an object placed in water will displace, or push away, some of that water. The water pushes back, and just how hard it pushes is determined by the amount of water displaced.

So when the barrel was full (the SS *Buttermilk*), it sank. The barrel pushed away water equal to its own size (or *volume*). But compared to the heavy barrel, this volume of water was not enough to keep the ship afloat.

And when the barrel was empty (the SS *Empty*), it did float, but was too light to push away nearly *any* water and made a terribly unstable ship.

But when the barrel was half full (the SS *Ballast*), it weighed just enough to push away the right amount of water to get the ship to float—*and* get safely to shore.

SIMON & SCHUSTER BOOKS FOR YOUNG READERS • An imprint of Simon & Schuster Children's Publishing Division • 1230 Avenue of the Americas, New York, New York 10020 • Text copyright © 2013 by Lynne Berry • Illustrations copyright © 2013 by Matthew Cordell • All rights reserved, including the right of reproduction in whole or in part in any form. • SIMON & SCHUSTER BOOKS FOR YOUNG READERS is a trademark of Simon & Schuster, Inc. • For information about special discounts for bulk purchases, please contact Simon & Schuster Special Sales at 1-866-506-1949 or business@simonandschuster.com. • The Simon & Schuster Speakers Bureau can bring authors to your live event. For more information or to book an event, contact the Simon & Schuster Speakers Bureau at 1-866-248-3049 or visit our website at www.simonspeakers.com. • Book design by Chloë Foglia • The text for this book is set in Horley Old Style. Hand lettering created by Matthew Cordell • The illustrations for this book are rendered in pen and ink with watercolor. Manufactured in China • 0413 SCP

2 4 6 8 10 9 7 5 3 1

Library of Congress Cataloging-in Publication Data • Berry, Lynne. • What floats in a moat? / by Lynne Berry ; illustrated by Matthew Cordell.—1st ed. • p. cm. • ISBN 978-1-4169-9763-4 (hardcover) • ISBN 978-1-4424-8131-2 (eBook) • Summary: While trying to cross a moat, Archimedes the Goat and Skinny the Hen learn why objects sink or float. • [1. Stories in rhyme—Fiction. 2. Floating bodies—Fiction. 3. Goats—Fiction. 4. Chickens—Fiction.] Cordell, Matthew, 1975– ill. • PZ8.3.B4593 Wh 2013 • [E] • 2010002844

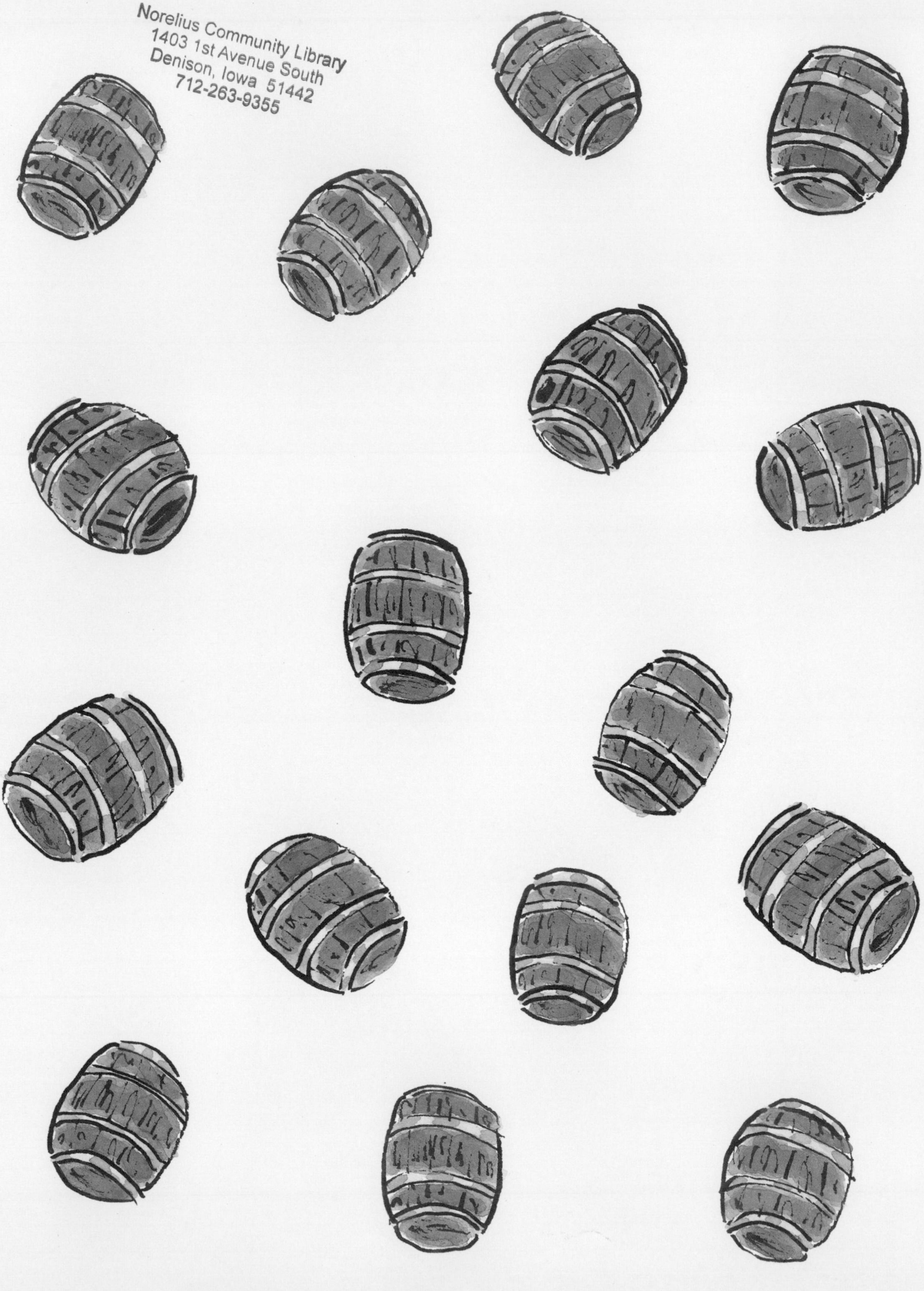